BABY'S HOUSE

By Gelolo McHugh

Illustrated by Mary Blair

A GOLDEN BOOK · NEW YORK

Here is Baby's door.
Let's open it.

This is Baby's room.

Here are Baby's toys.

This is the window Mother opens.

Baby has a dressing table,
with a mirror to look in.
Baby has a high chair to sit in, too.

Baby has a bright red ball.
Baby can roll the ball.

Good-by, Baby's room.
Now let's open this door.

Oh, here is the bathroom.
Here is the tub where Baby swims.

This is Baby's cup.
This is Baby's big, soft towel.

And here are the toothbrush

and the soap.

Good-by, bathroom.

Here is another door to open.

See the kitchen.
Here is the stove.
See Baby's dinner cooking.

Here is the sink.

This is the refrigerator.
It is cold inside.
Baby's milk is in the refrigerator.

Good-by, kitchen.

Let's open another door.

This is the living room.

Here is the table.
And there is a clock.
Tick tock, tick tock.

Here is the big chair.
Here is the lamp beside it.

Come with us, puppy.
We are going out.
Good-by, living room.

Close the front door.

This is the front porch.

Good night, House.